The Sun's Daughter

To my sisters
—P.S.

For Jamal Jackson—your friendship was such
beautiful sunshine when times were gray
—R.G.C.

Clarion Books · a Houghton Mifflin Company imprint · 215 Park Avenue South, New York, NY 10003 · Text copyright © 2005 by Patrice Sherman · Illustrations copyright © 2005 by R. Gregory Christie · The illustrations were executed in gouache, acrylic, and tempera paint. The text was set in 18-point Mrs. Eaves Roman. · All rights reserved. · For information about permission to reproduce selections from this book, write to Permissions, Houghton Mifflin Company, 215 Park Avenue South, New York, NY 10003·

www.houghtonmifflinbooks.com

Manufactured in China

Library of Congress Cataloging-in-Publication Data
Sherman, Pat.
The sun's daughter : a story based on an Iroquois legend / by Pat Sherman ; illustrated by R. Gregory Christie. · p. cm.
ISBN 0-618-32430-5 (alk. paper)1. Iroquois Indians—Folklore. 2. Tales—New York (State) I. Christie, Gregory, 1971-, ill. II. Title. · E99.I7S515 2004 · 398.2′.089′9755—dc22
2004017820

ISBN-13: 978-0-618-32430-9   ISBN-10: 0-618-32430-5

SCP 10 9 8 7 6 5 4 3 2 1

the Sun's Daughter

by Pat Sherman

Illustrated by R. Gregory Christie

Clarion Books · New York

Once upon a time, the people of the earth did not have to dig or plant or hoe or reap, for the Sun had sent her own daughter Maize to walk among them. And wherever tall, golden Maize walked, tall stalks bearing golden grain grew. So the people had only to reach up in order to eat.

5

Maize loved the earth so much that she called for her sisters Pumpkin and Red Bean to join her. Soon bright orange pumpkins and scarlet beans bloomed amid the golden stalks. All day, the three sisters sang as they worked, and the wind carried their sweet voices across the fields and far into the forest.

The Sun felt pleased with her daughters and smiled upon the earth. But she warned them, "Stay in the open fields where I can see you. Don't go near the forest or down among the rocks and caves."

Both Pumpkin and Red Bean were humble little girls and they bent low to the ground. "Yes, Mother," they murmured.

But Maize, tall and slender, tossed her head in the wind. "Why should I stay in the open fields with my sisters?"

When their mother had gone to sleep for the night, Maize still shone her golden light upon the earth. She could not sleep but swayed restlessly with every breeze. "Surely I am old enough to walk where I wish."

Alone, she strolled to the edge of the forest, her golden skin lighting the path before her. Farther and farther she wandered. Suddenly, two sharp, glittering sparks flashed out at her. Silver, with his piercing eyes, peered from the entrance of his cave. Maize leapt back.

"Please." His voice hissed, icy as sleet. "I heard you and your sisters singing. I saw your golden light. Please, I am so lonely in my home underground. Do not run away."

Maize hesitated.

"Please." Tears froze on Silver's pale cheeks. "Please," he whispered. "I am so cold."

He looked so beautiful and sad standing there in the darkness
that Maize reached out.

"Please . . ."

Her fingertips grazed his arm, his neck, his chest. Wherever
she touched, his silver skin became warm as her gold.

So they stayed all night beneath the trees at the mouth of the
cave, pale Silver and golden Maize.

When morning came, the Sun gazed down at the earth once more. She saw plump, pretty Pumpkin and sweet, skinny Bean. "Where is your elder sister?" she asked. Pumpkin and Red Bean could not answer.

Deep in the forest, Maize woke. "Pumpkin and Red Bean must already be up and in the fields," she thought. "The people are hungry."

She jumped to her feet. "My mother will be looking for me," she told Silver.

But Silver seized her in his strong arms, chilling her to the bone. "Please! You cannot go!"

"Where is Maize?" the Sun demanded. Pumpkin and Red Bean withered and fainted under their mother's wrath. The Sun thrust her face close to the earth. She examined every blade of grass, turning it over and over until nothing was left in the fields. But Maize could not be found on the ground.

The Sun peered among the leaves of the trees, rubbing each one until it was brittle and brown. But Maize could not be found in the forest. The Sun even drank all the pools and rivers dry. But Maize could not be found under the water.

"Where is my daughter?"

The people panted and sweated beneath the Sun's rage, but they could not answer.

Finally, the Sun turned her face away, calling Pumpkin and Red Bean to her. "Neither I nor any of my children shall touch the earth until Maize returns."

Slowly the sky became gray. The ground grew white. The trees turned to stone. The birds shivered and flew up to the arms of the Sun.

But the people could not fly. They only grew weaker and thinner.

"Please," they begged the Sun. "We are so cold."

But the Sun would not touch the earth, even with her fingertips.

"Please. We will wither and shrivel. Our bellies are empty and turn to stone."

But the Sun would not look at them, even for a moment.

Now, among all the tribes of birds there was one that, though small, was braver than all the rest. These little gray pewee birds took pity upon the people. "We will find Maize," they told the Sun.

Banding together, they began their long journey back to the earth. Singing all the time to cheer one another on, they circled the fields, the forests, the rocks, and the streams. Deep in Silver's cave, Maize heard the birds, and their song reminded her so much of her sisters that she sang, too, like an echo rising from the darkness. The birds sang and Maize answered, each note drawing the pewees closer and closer to the mouth of the cave, until they flew fearlessly right into the cave itself. There they found Maize, held by jealous Silver.

"Please." The birds explained how the ground had turned white and the trees to stone. "The people wither and grow hungrier each day. The Sun will not touch them unless Maize returns."

"Please," Maize begged Silver. "If you let me see my mother and sisters again, I promise I will come back to you. Let me go for a year."

But Silver would not listen.

"Then for only half the year."

"No," he told her. "I will not let you go until . . . until the trees weep." For he knew the trees had turned to stone and could not weep.

Maize thought of the cold, bare trees. "But if they ever did weep," she insisted, "would you keep your word?"

"Yes," he replied. "I would keep my word and let you go for half the year."

Maize turned to the birds. "Please." Her eyes filled with tears. "Can you make the trees weep for me?"

The pewees were not discouraged. They sped from the cave and fluttered among the cold, hard branches. "Please weep," they begged first one tree, then another. "Please weep." Their small voices filled the empty forest. "Please weep. Please weep." They shivered and trembled but would not leave. "Please weep. Please weep."

The Sun heard the birds. "I said I would not touch the earth until Maize returns," she thought. "But perhaps it would do no harm to touch just the tops of the trees." She stretched out her arms and gently, lightly, softly brushed the tips of the uppermost branches of the trees.

"Please weep!"

The Sun's warmth penetrated to the trees' very roots.

"Please weep!"

And slowly, one by one, the trees began to weep. Shining tears of silver and gold trickled down their rough bark. When the people saw the tears, they reached out to taste. The tears of the birch and pine tasted bitter, like those of the people. But when they came to the maple tree, they found that the tears were sweet. They remembered the voices of Maize, Pumpkin, and Red Bean singing in the fields. Sweet.

"Even the trees weep!" They stared at each other in wonder. "The trees weep."

25

True to his word, Silver released Maize. "But for only half the year," he reminded her. "For without you I am so lonely and cold."

Maize sped from the cave, her long legs traveling in great leaps. With each step, the ground beneath her feet became soft and green.

The people ran to greet her. Pumpkin and Red Bean danced in their orange and scarlet skirts. The Sun smiled upon the earth.

"But you must all help now," Maize told the people. "For I will be among you only half the year."

And that is how the people learned to bend their backs to dig and hoe, to get down on their knees to plant and weed. At the end of the half-year, they gave a feast in honor of Maize. They bound golden stalks together, in tall towers throughout the fields. And this was the last thing Maize saw upon the earth as she looked over her shoulder before she rejoined her lover Silver deep in his cave.

So each year, to this day, when Maize leaves the earth, the ground becomes white, the trees turn to stone, and the birds fly up to the arms of the Sun.

But just when you think Maize will never return, the bravest and smallest of the birds fly homeward and you can hear them dancing in the branches, begging the trees, "Please weep!"

Author's Note

Stories of the Corn Maiden and other harvest goddesses are told by many cultures throughout the world. Ancient Greeks called her Persephone. In northern Europe, people honored the changing seasons by creating straw figures of the Corn Maiden and burning them at the end of the harvest season. The Hopi and Pueblo tribes of the southwestern United States still recount the legend of the Blue Corn Maiden, who was captured by the spirit of winter when she wandered too far from her home. The spirits of winter and summer then fought over her until she agreed to spend half the year with each, bringing peace and abundance back to the earth.

The Sun's Daughter is an original story. It was inspired by the Iroquois tales of the Corn Maiden—Maize—and her sisters Pumpkin and Red Bean. The Iroquois form one of the largest native tribes in eastern United States and Canada. They introduced the first European settlers to their crops and also taught them how to gather sweet sap from the maple tree.

The pewee bird is also a native of northeastern America. It was no doubt a familiar and comforting presence to both peoples. Small and gray, pewees are among the first migrators to arrive each spring. Their low, gentle notes, *peeeweeht, peeweeht,* can almost sound like "please weep" if you listen carefully enough.